Albert Liked Ladders

First published 2005
Evans Brothers Limited
2A Portman Mansions
Chiltern Street
London WIU 6NR

British Library Cataloguing in Publication Data
Swallow, Su
          Albert liked ladders. – (Twisters)
          1. Children's stories – Pictorial works
          I. Title
          823.9'14 [J]

ISBN 0237529300
13-digit ISBN (from 1 January 2007) 9780237529307

Printed in China by WKT Company Limited

Series Editor: Nick Turpin
Design: Robert Walster
Production: Jenny Mulvanny
Series Consultant: Gill Matthews

Albert Liked Ladders

Su Swallow
and Barbara Nascimbeni

Evans

Albert liked ladders.

He liked ladders going up...

8

...and down.

But no one would let him climb their ladders.

"It's too high."

13

"Too wobbly!"

14

"Too dangerous!"

16

"Too windy!"

19

"Too dark."

21

"Too slippery."

"Too old."

25

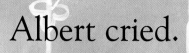

Albert cried.

"Follow me," said Dad.

"I've made a ladder just for you!"

Why not try reading another Twisters book?